ARMADILLO RODEO

WRITTEN AND ILLUSTRATED BY

JAN BRETT

SCHOLASTIC INC.

NEW YORK TORONTO LONDON AUCKLAND SYDNEY

For Jason Merrill

ISBN 0-590-22298-8

12 11 10 9 8 7 6 5 4 3 2 1   6 7 8 9/9 0 1/0

Printed in the U.S.A.   08

First Scholastic printing, September 1996

Armadillos, one, two, three—Bo! Let's go," Ma Armadillo called to her boys as they headed out to dig, deep in the heart of Texas hill country.

"Stay close!" Her boys didn't see too well, just like all armadillos, and she didn't want to lose them, especially Bo, who was always wandering off.

"One, two, three—Bo! Don't go gettin' distracted on me." But Bo already was. He was looking at a lizard.

Curious as always, Bo followed the lizard down to Can Creek just as Harmony Jean came sliding down the bank from the Curly H, wearing her brand-new boots—pointy-toed, high-heeled, hand-tooled, chili-pepper red boots with fancy cutwork, tall tops, and a Curly H brand. She was here to scuff them up. Today was rodeo day, and Harmony Jean was not about to ride in a barrel race looking like a tenderfoot in new boots.

She found a muddy place and hopped and splashed until her boots had a worn, lived-in look. Pleased, she whooped and hollered, "Look at me! Won't you just look at me!"

Bo's ears perked up at the sound of that pretty voice. He lifted his head and squinted. What he saw was all that red leather shimmering and prancing over the creek bed. Why, for sure, it looked to Bo as if he'd found a friend, a rip-roarin', rootin'-tootin', shiny red armadillo! Bo grinned. "Howdy!" he shouted.

Harmony Jean, job done, lit off through the back forty to the Curly H. Bo never looked back. He blinked and squinted as he trundled after his bright red friend as fast as he could go. "Wait up!" he called.

Back at the creek, his mama twitched an ear. "Is that hollerin' one of my boys?" she asked.

"Armadillos! One, two, three—Oh no, Bo!" He'd done it again.

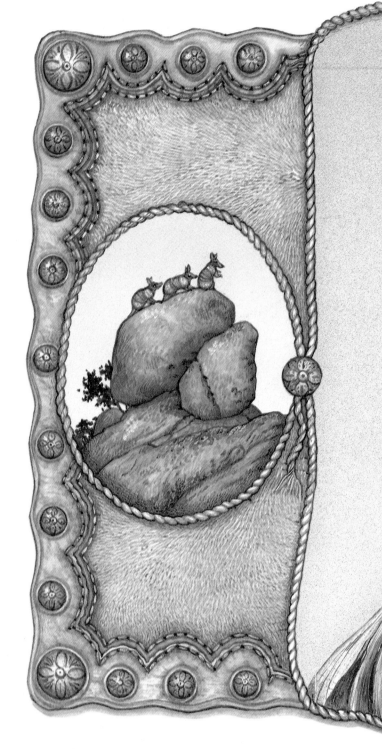

Bo arrived at the rodeo just as Harmony Jean was swinging a leg up on her pony, Spotlight. He saw the perky nose and silvery tail of the red armadillo leaping up ahead of him.

"Wait for me!" Bo called.

When Spotlight felt Bo on his back, he gave a hopping buck. Harmony Jean stayed aboard, but Bo was tossed high in the air. The little armadillo landed in the dust. As he unrolled, he smiled, brushed himself off, and shouted, "Hey, pardner! You're my kind of friend!"

Bo tried to catch sight of that rootin'-tootin' red armadillo, but he had to move fast. As he zigged and zagged across the arena, Ma Armadillo, with her three boys, was hot on his trail, asking everyone she met if they'd seen her Bo.

Bo was still looking when he saw the armadillo headed for the Bar-B-Q. "I'm right behind you," Bo called.

But before he could catch up, the armadillo disappeared under the blue-checked tablecloth. Bo dove after him and peered around. His friend was nibbling on something green, so Bo ambled over and took a big bite. It was a red-hot, bright-green jalapeño pepper.

His mouth on fire, Bo ran out and doused his head in lemonade to stop the burn. "Delicious," he gulped. "What's next?"

Chow time over, the cowhands got out their fiddles and everyone went into the barn for a little dancing. Bo struggled to see his pal. Finally he spotted a flash of red, right in the middle of all those stomping feet. Bo two-stepped toward his frisky new friend and cut in.

Harmony Jean went tap-slide-tap with her right foot, then heel-stomped, high-kicked with her left, and Bo was hurled high in the air. As he landed in the hayloft, he let out a rebel yell: "Yaaa-Hoo!"

Not far away, Ma Armadillo heard the commotion. "That's my Bo," she cried.

By the time Bo made it down the hay chute, the dance floor was empty. Harmony Jean and her friends had settled around the campfire. She looked down at her boots. They were starting to pinch. She slipped them off and tossed them behind her.

Bo bounded up to a pointy-toed, high-heeled, hand-tooled, chili-pepper red boot. "Howdy," he said. "You're a mighty hard fellow to keep up with. My name's Bo. What's yours?" His new friend didn't answer.

Bo stepped even closer. He could see the perky nose and the shy smile. "What's next?" he asked.

But instead of answering, his friend fell over, *plop*, and Bo was left looking down an opening. He stuck his head in and sniffed. It didn't smell like an armadillo. He poked his nose against the leather. It didn't feel like an armadillo. He squinted up close. It didn't even look like an armadillo. Nose in the air, he wailed, "You're not an armadilloooooooo!"

Not far away, the sharp ears of his ma recognized the voice of her boy. His three brothers heard him too. Their search was over. "Boys, let's go get Bo and head on home."

"Time to sleep, Bo," his ma said. "We have to go out and dig tomorrow."

"Yes, Ma."

But Bo's thinking about the Curly H. He knows that whenever he wants a change, he can mosey on down for some red-hot chili-pepper excitement and his ma will always be there to bring him home.